W9-BUP-222

BROOK TROUT
and the Writing Life

BOOKS BY CRAIG NOVA

Turkey Hash

The Geek

Incandescence

The Good Son

The Congressman's Daughter

Tornado Alley

Trombone

The Book of Dreams

The Universal Donor

Brook Trout and the Writing Life

BROOK TROUT
and the Writing Life

CRAIG NOVA

THE LYONS PRESS

Two short sections of this book appeared, in greatly different form, in *The New York Times Magazine* and *Men's Journal.*

Printed in the United States of America

10 9 8 7 6 5 4 3 2 1

Design by Compset, Inc.

Library of Congress Cataloging-in-Publication Data
Nova, Craig.
    Brook trout and the writing life / Craig Nova.
        p.   cm.
    ISBN 1-55821-974-9 (hc.)
    1. Brook trout fishing Anecdotes.   2. Nova, Craig.   I. Title.
SH689.3.N68   1999
799.1'7554—dc21   99-30595
                                                                        CIP

For
HOWARD MOSHER

I think it is all a matter of love: the more you love a memory, the stronger and stranger it is.

—Vladimir Nabokov

BROOK TROUT
and the Writing Life

One

I

*O*ften, the connection between things is not obvious to the eye, and even when it is, it can take years, if not decades, for me to see just what is associated with what. The events of my life and brook trout often meet at the line of demarcation between the world of the fish and the world of the fisherman, between the seen and the unseen. This division will be the surface of a stream, which I imagine, from the fish's point of view, as a silvery horizon, but which I see as a green sheet. Still, the moment of illumination has often come here, with a trout taking a fly out of the boundary between its world and mine.

For instance, I caught my first brook trout not long after my father died. One of my earliest memories is of my mother and father looking around at the flowers and trees they had planted in the yard of the house where I grew up in Hollywood,

California—lemon trees, boxwood, camellias, hibiscus, and sweet peas. My father had planted Victory gardens during the Second World War, before I was born, and I remember, too, that he spent an enormous amount of time trying to force four saplings he had planted so as to grow into the shape of a chair, until, defeated by their contrariness, or their wildness, he gave up. He told me that one dawn, when he had been up early, he had seen the light from atomic explosions in Nevada, four hundred miles to the east. He was not a fisherman, and I think he hated the out-of-doors in the way that I enjoy it. For him, the natural world, while profoundly beautiful, was an adversary more than anything else. We shared a sense of beauty, but where he wanted to control, I wanted to participate. My father died when I was in my late twenties.

I caught my first brook trout because of a woman I met at a party in New York City. Like all chance meetings that turn out differently than one supposes, I almost did not go to this party. It was downtown, in Soho, when it was illegal to live there, and the entire existence of many people had a furtive, almost hidden quality, as though they were doing something wrong. From time to time, people got put out on the street, but mostly they thrived, hidden from sight like trout lurking against a bank, or in the rubble of a stream.

The party was given by an illustrator who had run away from Arkansas, where he had grown up, to Chicago, where he got his start—if this is what one can call it—in a tattoo parlor. Often, people came into the tattoo parlor and looked over the ready-made designs without seeing one they wanted, and the illustrator's first job was to be able to provide, on the spot, just what it was the customer wanted but didn't see. One customer wanted to have Elmer Fudd tattooed on an exceedingly intimate spot. The illustrator used to tell this story with a smile and a shrug, as though this tattoo was a hint at how the ridiculous has its own insistence, and that fate has an instinct not only for wars and brutality, but for people sitting on wedding cakes, too.

Of course, memories come with varying intensity. A doctor once told me that a good question to ask, when trying to diagnose alcoholism, is this: "Can you remember your first drink?" A real drunk will be able to remember the moment with perfect clarity, the occasion, the clothes he wore, the smell of perfume, the time of day. In particular, he will remember the light. The real drunk will recall this moment with a sense of recognition. I have never had a problem with alcohol, and on those occasions years ago when I killed brook trout to eat, I liked to have them with new potatoes and a glass of dark beer. But I understand this sense of recognition, and it came at this party when I met the woman who was responsible for me catching my first brook trout.

At the time, she was working for television news. She was blond, about five feet five, and she was wearing a red sweater. She stood in a light that seemed bright and warm. We only talked for a couple of moments, which were awkward, since I had arrived at the wrong time at this party and in general it was somewhat trying. I went home early and forgot about it, although from time to time I recalled that light, that blond hair, and the red sweater. A smile and a kind of spunk, too. After all, she had started as an assistant cameraman, which in those days was not an easy thing for a woman to do. I imagined her hanging out of a helicopter with a sixteen-millimeter camera over one shoulder.

In those days, I was living in New York, doing my best to live up to the idea of just what a young novelist did when he wasn't writing, which, I found out, was a lot of the time, but this didn't mean I was getting much fishing in. Every now and then I would go down Minetta Lane, under which or near which, or so I had heard, ran Minetta Brook. It is hard for me to say why the notion of a brook so haunted me, but it did, and not just because it was in Manhattan, but because of the promise the word *brook* always suggested.

The fishing I had gotten in, before coming to New York, was limited to California. I remember a fishing trip when four or five teenage boys, myself included, had gone into the Sierras. We weren't great fishermen, and, in fact, I am not sure what the point of this trip was. We found a ranger who gave us a map with a wilderness section marked off, and in the middle of it there was a pond. The ranger pointed to the rectangle of wilderness and said, with an almost exquisite ignorance of adolescent

6

boys, "Don't go there." As soon as he left, we started in that direction. The pond didn't look so far away, but then, what did we know then about maps and distance?

We didn't get there until it was almost dark, and by then we were good and lost, since we didn't know for sure if the small lake we had found was the one we had wanted to go to. At six or seven thousand feet, it started to get cold as the sun went down.

One of us, but only one, had had the foresight to stick a can of tuna fish in his pocket, and the rest of us caught him where he had slinked off to eat it. We managed to get out in the morning, not quite as certain as we had been just a day or two before of how benign the natural world really was. This was a healthful shock, since until this moment all of us had the notion of the natural world as something out of a documentary about bears. None of us felt good about the experience, since up there, when we had been alone, it became apparent that we weren't such good friends after all. I had to wait for real friends until I came east. Many of them are associated with brook trout.

The woman in the red sweater and I met again. She made me dinner in her apartment. When we were sitting in her living room she told me that when she had been growing up she spent summers on a lake in New Hampshire where there were loons, and to demonstrate what they sounded like, she put her hands together and made their call. I listened and thought, "This could be trouble."

She said that she had a house in the country. Would I like to go sometime? She also told me that there was a stream on the land, too, and later I found out that it was called Fish Cabin. When I first heard this, I thought that surely this was a good sign, although years of bitter experience with the names of water like this has given me a more healthy skepticism than when I first heard the phrase "Fish Cabin." But I was in my twenties then and had a lot to learn.

2

On the night we were supposed to go to this woman's country place, we argued bitterly. We were going to leave on a Friday night, and she told me that she had something to do for work, and that this involved going to a party. I was supposed to rent a car and then park it in front of my apartment, where I would wait. She would call me, and then I would pick her up about ten in the evening. Then we would go to the place in the country, where there was a stream called Fish Cabin.

I rented the car. I parked it on the street, and then went to my apartment. An hour passed. Then two. At ten o'clock, the hour when we were supposed to leave, she called. I could hear the dance music in the background. She said it wouldn't be more than an hour more. She would leave then. Fine, fine, I said. I paced around in my apartment, a small place on Sullivan Street above a candy store. My small bath was above the pay phone downstairs, at which the loan shark who worked out of the store used to make his business calls, every word of which I could hear. I started the day shaving and listening to him go through his serial threatening, one after another, just like a carpenter driving nails. "You didn't have it on Monday, and you didn't have it on Tuesday, and this is Thursday. Do you understand what I'm telling you?"

The phone rang an hour later.

"I'm going to be a little while longer," she said.

"Okay," I said. "Fine. Call me."

"It can't be too much longer," she said.

"Why can't you leave now?" I said. "It's just a party. It's not like you are shooting film, is it?"

"I'll call you later," she said. "Not more than an hour."

"I'll be here," I said.

I hung up. I idly thought about the things that had happened to the people who hadn't understood what the loan shark had been telling them. The clock showed one in the morning, then two. I looked out the window where I could see the car I had rented.

The phone rang.

"It can't be too much longer," she said. "Really. I mean it."

"All right," I said.

I waited another hour. She called again.

"I'm almost ready to go," she said.

"Look," I said. "I really have no business saying anything about what you do."

"What do you mean?" she said.

Old rock and roll in the back ground. The Rolling Stones. Otis Redding.

"You know, it's hard for me to hear," she said. "The music is so loud."

"I said that you can do whatever you want but don't keep me waiting around while you do it," I said. Right then I thought, That's it. We don't know each other well enough to argue like this. I glanced out the window at the car. Maybe if I took it right back they might give me a refund. That was about the best I could expect. Why couldn't I just say nothing?

More rock and roll music.

"I think we should talk about this," she said.

"When do you think we should talk about it?" I said. "In another hour?"

"What?" she said. "I can't hear you. Listen. I'll be at my apartment in an hour. All right?"

"Okay," I said.

I hung up, took off my clothes, and got into bed. Screw it. If they start treating you like that in the beginning, what can you expect later? Isn't this just a matter of reaching down and taking my courage with both hands, as they say in Spain? I sat there in the dark. Then I got up and dressed and took my bag.

She was waiting in front of her building. It must have been four in the morning, and since it was early summer, the sky in the east began to have that silky gray quality, like sheer underwear. She got in. I drove.

"You drive very well," she said.

"Uh-huh," I said.

"Look, I'm sorry, okay?" she said.

We sat at a deserted intersection, the light against us. No cars. Damp streets. Manhattan before dawn. I was thinking of Minetta Brook, of the water that ran deeply concealed there, of the years I had spent in the city away from such things as brooks.

"So, are you coming with me or staying here?" she said.

I looked at the cold sheen of the street in front of us.

"Well?" she said.

"I'm coming. How do I get there?" I said.

She moved closer, sliding across the seat. It made a little sound.

"Take the tunnel," she said. "I'll show you."

3

The land was about two hours away from New York, on the Delaware River above Port Jervis. We drove through New Jersey and over some low mountains and then down to the Delaware

River, where I would catch a lot of fish, but I didn't know that then. What I saw was the broad, gray expanse of the water, mirrorlike against the land at dawn. We drove along it for a while, passing a stream called the Mongaup, which ran under the road to the Delaware. This, I found out later, was great brook trout water, and even now I can remember the boulders at the head of the pool just behind which the trout hung in the evening, taking an endless supply of white mayflies. If you timed it right, you could stand there for an hour or so before dark and catch one brookie after another—good-sized ones, too, twelve inches. Through the clear water I often saw them finning, tailing as they pushed their noses through the rubble, looking for nymphs.

"Turn here," she said.

The dirt road went up a hill and then flattened out, running between woods on one side and a field on the other. The field was surrounded by stone walls. We kept going, the road running through white oak and rock oak, although all I could see at the time was the shaggy shapes of trees emerging from the dark.

The house we came to was a small green one with white trim. It had two stories, and it was in a small yard enclosed by stone walls. In front of it four apple trees grew. The house had clapboards, a small porch. Beyond it there was a field surrounded by woods. We parked the car and went in, to the musty smell of a house that has been closed up for a couple of weeks.

In the bedroom upstairs the light of dawn was just coming through the window. We slept late, waking in that same smell of a house that had been empty but needed to have someone live in it.

Everything about this piece of land had a sense of being abandoned. It had been bought by the woman's grandfather, and he had run it as a gentleman's farm. The grandfather was dead now, and a thousand acres of it had been sold. What was left were a few hundred acres, the green house, which had been a place where farmers had lived a hundred years before, and another building, a stone house that was down in the woods, on the way to Fish Cabin.

To get to the stream, you had to walk down a road that slowly vanished into what was an old wood road, but time had made it elegant. The road seemed to have the aspect of a bower, since it was overtopped with ash and oak, and the enclosed aspect of it had a regularity, too. If you were on your way down to Fish Cabin, it looked as though you were going through a formal garden, or one that was a little more wild than that, like Monet's. The wood road led to a seep where watercress grew, and if you followed the rill of water, with the scent of watercress in the air, and went more steeply downhill, you came to the stream itself. The air of the hillside was at once dusty and ominous, but this was instantly relieved at the bottom where the water pooled up on the ledges.

Fish Cabin was not a large stream, but it ran through a steep and rocky landscape, which made the stream into a series of falls. On the ledges between them, the water almost always formed a pool. A few of these were twenty or so feet across, and some were narrower. A couple of pools were deep, filled with green water on which there was a white and silver fluff where the stream emptied into it.

After we had been coming here for a couple of weekends, the woman who brought me to this land said, "Here. I'd like you to have this."

Her name was Christina. She passed over a tube in which there was a fly rod, a new bamboo one. A reel, too.

The fishing I had done in the West had been done with a spinning outfit, but I had always had a romantic idea of casting flies for trout. I had an image in my mind, perhaps from an other era, of men false casting long lines over water that was just about to fall to a pool below. Now, I played around with the fly rod on the lawn. I bought some flies. Some nymphs, too. Some Adams, and some weighted Hare's Ears, gold-ribbed ones that had been tied with a spinning loop so that in the water they would be lifelike and buggy, the color of the rubble on the bottom of Fish Cabin.

We came to the green house as often as we could. Of course, we usually arrived late at night. The creaking of the house, as it lost heat, gave us a sense of it almost being alive. In those days, we often brought a picnic from a delicatessen downtown in New York, and sometimes we had a snack with the sun about to rise, licking our fingers and talking a little bit.

One Saturday morning I got up early and went out with the fly rod. It was foggy when I got to the wood road, and when I came to the seep, the mist in the woods was filled with slanting rays of light as you might see in a dusty room, the lines defined by the long streaks of shadows made by the spruce and hemlock that grew on the steep sides of the hill. I followed the rill. In the mist, which was a little cool, and in that light, which came in as though through a cathedral window, I thought of the warmth of the space under the blanket where Christina was sleeping.

In those days, I didn't really know what I was doing in the fishing department, but at least I had some notion of the theoretical aspects of catching fish on a fly. I remember not being very certain about the length of a leader, particularly for nymph fishing. Still, I got down to the stream, and what I remember is the light coming through the mist in those long shadows, and the way in which the trunks of the spruce were covered with a gold film. The sound of the stream was constant, but somehow just irregular enough to keep it from being machinelike.

I stood at the top of a pool and flicked the nymph here and there, looking at the mist and smelling the odor of hemlock in it. What I remember about catching my first brook trout was that ominous tug of it: sudden, serious, with all the purpose that millions of years of evolution can bring to one small act.

I had a little creel with me in those days, which just goes to show how romantic I was then. The brook trout had dark squiggles on its back, a line of red dots on its side, and when I touched it, the fish's skin had a silky touch to it, not slimy, but more like the softest leather imaginable. Its eyes were dark, looking out at me from a more demanding world than the one I was living in. Ferns grew by the brook, and I picked a few and put them in the creel and put the fish in, too, where I saw the gray sparkle and red dots of a brook trout's flanks.

About ten in the morning, when I came back to the house, Christina was drinking coffee and wearing her grandfather's bathrobe. Her grandfather had been a great fisherman, and while he had been tough about a lot of things, he had owned a terry cloth bathrobe, which Christina now liked to wear. She was sleepy, her hair in her face. When I showed her the creel, with the ferns and trout, she put her coffee cup down and pushed her hair out of her face with both hands. Her grandfather's bathrobe didn't have a sash, and to look into the basket she had to let the front panels swing open so she could see the brook trout.

We started coming to this house almost every weekend now, arriving late, getting away from the city, which seemed to exist as a mosaic, the tiles of it made of squares of light, some of them a little blue, like the rings around the spots on a brook trout. We came into the house with a picnic, primed the pump in the cellar, turned on the icebox. We planned to get married, and then we did. We kept coming to the house.

4

The next spring, in those complicated impulses that I felt after the death of my father, I suggested that we plant a garden. In the field just beyond the house, there was a fenced-in patch, and we turned over the soil by hand, mixed in some fertilizer, and planted the kinds of vegetables my father must have put into a Victory garden. I even found myself looking at four saplings, spaced like chair legs, growing in the woods, but this was a momentary ache, and if nothing else, the fact that I left them alone means that something valuable, if only by inverse example, is passed from father to son.

I still went into Fish Cabin now, and in the depths of summer when it was hot, Christina came with me. We went to a pool in the middle of the stream, which was halfway between the flat land at the top of a gorge and the bottom, where the stream flowed into the Delaware. In between there was a drop of about five hundred feet, and it was hard to get into this section because the sides of the gorge were steep.

At the bottom of the gorge, the brook wasn't fished very often. Not only was it hard to get to, but people believed that there were a lot of copperheads down here. The snakes were supposed to like the ledges, the rubble of fieldstone, and the speckled shade here at noon on a summer's day. Later, when I ran this piece of land as a tree farm, one of the foresters I worked with said he wouldn't go into Fish Cabin because of the snake problem.

The pool that I liked the best was deep, with boulders at the head. I got to it by following the water that ran out of a damp place on the hillside. In the middle of summer, the pool was cool, and often in the shade. The hemlock and spruce were large here, and under them rhododendron grew, their leaves having a sheen in the dark green shade. The water itself was silvery where the stream came into the pool, and then it seemed green in the shade of the spruce and hemlock.

Now, when I came to this place, Christina came with me, and when she did, she brought along a hammock, which she hung between some trees. When I fished, she got into the hammock, which was screened by some leaves, and slept, one arm languidly emerging from the shadows into a patch of light. I fished from the head of the pool, making contact now and then, and looking up to see that arm, the thin wrist, the open hand which rested now in the shade and in the mist that came up from the surface of the water. Further up, on one of the next ledges, which were arranged like steps, I saw the sheet of water that washed out on the stone and then fell into the pool that I fished.

After these afternoons, we'd climb up the bank, being careful where we put our hands, and in those days, I'd bring some trout home for lunch, the weight of them bananalike against my side in a bag I carried. Christina followed, sometimes with leaves or a little clutter in her hair, both of us going up between the trunks of hemlocks. We passed the seep where the watercress grew, and took some of that, too, to make a salad to go with the trout.

I also dug some new potatoes from the garden, and we sautéed them with butter and had them with parsley. The brook trout were so fresh they squirmed in the pan, and we had them with a glass of dark beer. Their flesh was pink, and the potatoes had the taste of the earth, and while I ate them, I thought of the gorge, of Christina's hand emerging from the shadows and the shiny leaves, the shape of the hammock hung there just where the trout couldn't see.

What I was thinking of, down below, when that tug of the fish came, was my father's attempt to make the saplings grow into a chair, and how I had not been the son I had wanted to be, and then I looked up at the shape of the hammock, into the mists, seeing Christina stir in her sleep. One often wonders what the precise moment of conception is, the instant when life begins, and I often think that she conceived, there in the depths, when I thought of how I missed my father, and in the moment I felt the tug of the fish. The tug was serious and implied the frankness of something that had been done for millions of years.

I never saw a copperhead by the stream or in the gorge, although we did see a timber rattler there, just once. There were copperheads around the house, and the farmers who had lived in the house before us used to take pieces of crockery and broken dishes and put them on top of the stone walls to keep the snakes from sunning themselves there.

We ate our trout and potatoes, and drank the beer, and Christina told me that she had been feeling sick in the mornings. Why was that, she wondered. I thought about the tug, the Victory garden, the light my father had seen from the atomic explosions, the haunting luminescence of which seemed to mix with the memory of a glow in that apartment in Soho. I liked to think, too, while I waited for the next moment, which I knew was surely going to come, of the brook trout in Fish Cabin, finning in the dark water where they waited, perfectly shaped to exist in the current.

Two

I

*W*ithout even realizing it, of course, I had begun to depend upon those times when I could go down to Fish Cabin, or the Mongaup, and spend a few hours. Mostly, what I was doing then, and what I still do on different water, is watch. Watching was my Harvard and my Yale. It took a long time to discover just what was happening in the water, and I am not sure I really have it yet. Surely, I have learned a trick or two and know the names of a few insects, and I have learned something about the length of leaders and the thickness, too, but all of this, which I learned so slowly and with such effort, came from watching. For instance, things were far more connected than I had thought in the beginning. Often, when Christina and I were at the green house, I went to the Delaware, or the Mongaup, or Fish Cabin, and on my way I saw hawks. When I saw them on a clear day, the fishing wasn't so good. It took me a little while to figure it out, but this was the way I discovered that brook trout, and other trout, too, are very concerned about shadows. Or, to be more specific, moving ones.

The beginning of trouble is often so perfectly disguised, so hard to see, that I don't even notice that it is there. Later, of course, when I am sifting through the wreckage, I can see it clearly. People have always tried to explain this up-and-down aspect of human existence, the ebb and flow of fortune. They have said that it is caused by hubris. A twist of fate. Chance. And, of course, none of this explains how things go wrong, or what one can do to guard against these moments, which by definition come as surprises and out of the places one least suspects them to be. In any true account of one's experience, and in mine with brook trout (or when and why I went fishing for them), it is necessary to confront such moments, which when I look back are a kind of moving shadow.

Christina and I were in the green house when we took out the pregnancy test we had bought at a pharmacy in New York and which we had brought along with the picnic from the downtown delicatessen. We followed the instructions. In those days you had to wait overnight to get the results, and I got up early and peered into the top of the device, at the bottom of which I saw a round O. This meant that we were going to have a child. Later in the day, I went down into Fish Cabin, since there was no way that I could feel how happy I was just sitting around. It was as though I had to be there in the mists and green light, the sound of the water, and the rush of it across the stones there to feel it.

Something went wrong, though, and I am not sure precisely what it was. I suppose it had to do with being a young novelist who was far too ambitious (ambition, at least, is an item I have learned to handle with caution), and then I suppose there was a lot of pressure to become well known or successful, or some other word that implied everything that is wrong about fame. I am not sure about what it was, but I know this. Something went wrong. Christina and I argued. In any marriage there is a time in which the people in it have to come to terms with just what it means to spend the rest of your life with someone, and this can be a shock. I think that it frightened us both.

I was waiting for a book to be published, and I found myself wandering around the country for a month. Christina was still at CBS News. When I came back, we were still not getting along well. But we were happy in a way, at moments, and certainly we were excited about having a child. The baby, Abbey, was born at night, on an evening when a snowstorm moved quickly through New York. A doctor at the hospital told me that amniotic fluid responds to changes in barometric pressure, and the abrupt drop of it with the quickly moving storm caused many women who were pregnant to go into labor. Through reasons of imprecise association, I immediately thought of the silver water in the gorge of Fish Cabin.

I was at the hospital all night. The baby was a healthy child, although a little early. It had snowed, and when I came out of the hospital the parking lot was covered with a couple of inches. It looked blue in the morning light. The morning was cold, and the sting of the air was, or so it seemed to me, the sensation of happiness itself.

When I got home an hour later I picked up the newspaper and found that the book I had just published had been given a very bad review. Or, more than that. The review had been written by a bitter man (now dead), and a bitter man has a way of seeing the world as an ugly place. What got to me, though, was that he may have been right, since there were a lot of other bad reviews, too. There is no silence like the silence that comes from a publisher when things are going badly. No paperback book sale. I was broke.

2

In the spring, my wife and I and our newborn child gave up our apartment in New York and moved to the green house. I had eleven hundred dollars in the world. What in god's name was I going to do?

I started a new book. In the evenings I went fishing for brook trout, and as I did so, watching them rise to the small white flies on the stream, the act of catching them was a matter of putting me in touch with something so definite as to give me the hope of being able to write. Of course, Christina and I were scared. We planted a garden, moved the things from our apartment into the house, unpacked our bags, tried to come to terms with what was wrong.

We argued bitterly, and there were times when I was so angry that I reached up to the low ceilings of the house and tried to lift it off the foundations. Then I would go down to the Mongaup. I began to read something about brook trout, about mayflies, caddis flies, stone flies. I wrote in the morning and then went to the river. I discovered more things. For instance, the Mongaup is a stream that has a dam on it, and from time to time, water is released from it without warning. There are many streams like this, and I have always felt an affection for them, the way one feels affection for some old danger. What I learned about them is this: The trout wait for the rise in water, because they know that when the water rises, it sweeps into the stream the beetles, grasshoppers, and other insects that are in the grass along the bank. When the water rises, the big fish move into pockets along the bank, and when they do so, they feed with a kind of greed.

I learned this the hard way. I was in the middle of the Mongaup, facing downstream, when the water began to rise. This always comes as a surprise on the Mongaup. There is no whistle, no sound at all aside from the change in the tempo of the sounds the stream makes. Then you look around and see that the water is coming up, and it is doing so very quickly. By chance, under these circumstances, I cast a stone fly, a big nymph (my entomology was coming along) against the bank, and instantly a large fish took it. So, there I was, in the middle of the stream, hooked to the biggest fish I had ever seen (not a brookie, but one of the enormous browns that had come up out of the Delaware), and as I tried to play him, the wall of water swept toward me. The choices were pretty obvious: Catch the fish and die or break off and live. I broke the fish off and started for the bank.

A writer once said that as you get older, you don't remember the romantic encounters you had so much as the ones you could have had and didn't take. I'd like to add that the same thing is true about fish, and even now, years later, I still think about this one that came up from the depths of the Delaware. Still, I have had good success fishing along the banks on streams where the water rises fast, although I am more careful about where I stand to do it.

Usually, whether on the Mongaup or in Fish Cabin or on the Delaware (and then on streams further away, the Lackawaxen, for instance, and the branches of the Delaware), I would fish until dark. When I came home, the kitchen light would be on. Christina would be there, reading at the table, looking up from her book when I came in the door. She'd smile. I would, too. We'd sit and have a drink. Sometimes our daughter was awake, and there were occasions when Christina had made an apple or a blueberry pie. The only sound was the crickets outside on those summer nights, the ticking of the house, and the quiet talk. We'd have a drink and watch as the deer came into the field—three of them—flicking their tails in the last light of dusk.

Eleven hundred dollars, even in those days, wasn't going to last very long. A friend told me about an editor in New York, a man who had had good luck publishing young writers. I decided to go see this man, and I put on a tie, shined my shoes, and drove to New York. I instantly liked him. He was smart and gracious, a lovely man. We talked over what had happened with my last book, and he said that if I brought him a part of the new book, he might be able to publish it. I went back to the green house. Christina and I were typing the new manuscript to take it to New York when someone called to tell me that the editor I had spoken to had died. He had died, the caller said, in the Fourteenth Street subway station. It had been, the caller said, "an ignominious" death.

Christina had been typing the pages when the call came. I told her the news.

"Oh, no," she said.

She took my hand. We stood there like two teenagers on a date. Our daughter began to cry.

"What are you going to do?" she said.

"I'm not sure," I said.

"We haven't got a lot of money left."

"I know," I said.

Christina picked up the baby. I held her, too, and I could still smell that odor that new babies have. Christina bit her lip. I knew that soon the crickets would start working outside, in the dark, the un-huh, un-huh like the sound of something unstoppable and ill-meaning. I looked down at the table on which there was a copy of a book I had been reading, Ray Bergman's *Trout*, on the cover of which there was a painting of a brook trout. It was painted from the trout's point of view, under the water, and the surface showed as a film on which some mayflies floated. A trout was getting ready to take one.

"All right," said Christina, as though acquiescing in some enormous thing, which, I suppose, was a refusal to panic. "Maybe you should go fishing tonight. We always seem to see things a little more clearly after you come back from the river."

3

One of the things that has always intrigued me is the way in which a fisherman can remember a stretch of water. Even now, years after fishing many streams, I can still remember how the water was laid out, where the boulders were, the shape of a pool and how it changed as the season advanced and the water levels rose or fell. For instance, there was a spot I fished regularly in June on the Mongaup. It was a deep pool. I used to start fishing from the tail, and when I faced upstream I saw the flat water of the middle of the pool (which, as the sun went down, was green, tinted with pink). At the head of the pool, on the right-hand side, there was a boulder that stuck up about five or six feet. The brook trout liked to hang in the water, just behind the boulder, so they could take the insects that were being washed down the stream. The fish were just far enough back from the fast current so that you could see the disruption of the surface when they took a fly, and in June, in the evening, this was usually a little blond one (what the Latin boys call a *Potomanthus distinctus*). When the trout took one, they made a little watery *snap*. Often I heard the sound before I saw the splash of a fish, and when I went home, walking up the bank in the dark where the fireflies had started to blink, I remembered that sound of the brook trout taking an insect.

In the evenings, we sat in the kitchen and looked out the window at the deer. Some people came up to the land around the green house to kill a deer out of season, and I didn't object, since I knew that there were hungry people in Port Jervis. Surely, if there were hungry people in town, I would have been willing to kill a deer myself, or a lot of them, so that the people in town could have something to eat.

In addition to hungry people, a couple of market poachers were working here, too. There was a man who hunted this piece of land regularly, and he often told me which restaurants were stretching out their hamburger with deer they had bought from market poachers. And then, too, there was a little business that had to do with the fact that many men were having affairs, and that the way they got to spend time with their girlfriends was during hunting season. They went off to an island or a motel with their girl-friends and then bought a deer from a market poacher so as to have the proof of where they had been for a week when they got home.

While we were trying to decide what to do, we cheered our-selves up, and any small thing seemed to help. For instance, I re-member telling Christina about a game warden I had become friendly with. I was never one of those fisherman who was out on the stream on opening day, since in this part of the world, the fishing isn't much good on April 1. I mentioned this to the game warden and he looked at me for a moment and said, "Yeah. Noth-ing really happens until the first of May. We open trout season April the first to give the poor bastards something to do."

In the evenings, I thought about brook trout, about their tails, which are square, and made of something that more than any-thing else resembles wet silk. Their shapes seem aerodynamic, or hydrodynamic—not bulletlike, but something far more efficient than that. Their coloring is haunting, jeweled, dark eyed, definite.

There is an odor to the water that seems to hold brook trout, and I tried to recall it.

4

I was uncertain about the book I was trying to write. The pages piled up, but there was something wrong. In any writer's life there is a make or break moment, or there may be a number of them, and while I didn't realize I was in the middle of one, I knew I had to face some facts. Tolstoy says somewhere that many authors write books, but few are ashamed of them, and while I don't want to present myself as an exception to this accurate summation, I wasn't overly pleased with my early books. It is hard to be precise about the errors of one's youth, if only because sometimes they pave the way for better things, as though error had a hidden blessing. I knew I was through with the early books, and yet the new book was right there, just at the tips of my fingers, bouncing off them like a football that can almost but not quite be caught. Why couldn't I do it? It was just words, wasn't it?

I hadn't ever been able to write about love. Of course, like many young writers, or many writers altogether, I had been able to write about sex, but this, I discovered, is a way of avoiding something critical. I had never written about the attachment of one human being for another that was large, definite, and had demands far beyond the merely sexual. I knew this was at the heart of my difficulty, and I knew, too, that it was time to grow up as a writer. My first book had been published when I was in my twenties, and I now thought that it had been a mistake to do this when I was so young and so uninformed. I had been hiding from the demands of love, in writing and in living. I realized that I had been afraid. I was still afraid. I sat alone in a room and looked at the pages I had written. Hands sweating. Money running out.

The first item, I think, that got me going was the realization that my daughter was going to read what I wrote. Of course, not at this time, but in ten or fifteen or twenty years, or more importantly, after I was dead and gone. Surely, under these circumstances, I wanted to leave her something she could depend upon. This seems like an ordinary thing for a writer, and I suppose it is, but it allowed me to begin to approach those subjects I had avoided: love for another human being with all its attendant imperatives and disasters.

There was another matter, too, which is that not only had the subject of the earlier novels been the work of someone who needed to grow up, the style had been bald and uninformed. And, if it is hard to say how the subject of the new book had changed, it is almost impossible to say how the style, or the sense of language, changed along with it. I know for sure that I read Ford Maddox Ford with a kind of devotion. In the same way that a fisherman can remember a piece of water that he has fished, a boulder here, a glide there, a run against a ledge, I can remember pieces of description from other writers that seemed to open a door for me. For instance, Ford Maddox Ford described a woman's eyes as having "the gray-blue color of the rubble on the bottom of a stream." This is a small thing, but as soon as I read it, I recognized the lack of beauty in my early books and was determined to do something about it.

The new book was set on the land where we were living and one of the characters in it was a woman who lived here.

When Christina and I first started coming to the green house, I had found some naturalist books, which had belonged to her grandmother, and I had spent a lot of time looking through them and wondering what it had been like for her, on this land, when she had lived here. I began to include, in the book I was writing, the naturalist diary of a woman who had lived on this land. I didn't know quite why I was doing this, but one day I included an entry for brook trout.

Brook trout are the most beautiful of fish. They are streamlined and quick moving, having tails that are the color of hickory bark and the texture of wet silk. There are delicate rays in the tails as well, ridges that are fine and symmetrical. It is the coloring, though, which distinguishes them. They are dark, either brown or a bluish brown on the back, and they are almost impossible to see from above unless there are shadows. On their sides, however, they are marked differently: The color of the back gives way to a silvery brown and then to a satinlike and dark silver which is spotted with circles of brown and light brown, which circles have the aspect of cut and polished hardwood, oak, chestnut oak, walnut, cherry, or very old woods of a lighter color which have been handled and waxed and rubbed into darkness—that of a dining room table, say, made before the revolution and used steadily. Below these dark spots there is a line of bright circles which are red or orange and bright, and they have the aspects of sequins, of a silver maple leaf in the late fall. So when you hold one in your hand or when you look at a brook trout, at the speckled sides with that surprising line of red dots, it is as though you are staring not only at the side of a fish but at some mystery as well. The coloring seems to imply the enclosure or the completeness of the streams, since the fish have that aspect, or suggestion of the forests and stones through which and over which the water flows. There is the quality of surprise in the spots of orange that one finds when walking and putting up a grouse in an otherwise bland landscape. When the brook trout are feeding or quietly finning in some deep current, their presence is aloof and indifferent, but not unkind. Brook trout, or *Salvelinus fontinalis*, spend their lives in fresh water, the adults spawning in the fall, usually returning to the same place in a pool or stream where they themselves were spawned. The trout like gravely beds at this time of the year, and this is so because eggs laid in gravel will be protected, washed clean, and less likely to be suffocated by silt. A female goes to a stretch of gravel and lays her eggs and the male follows, covering them with his milt. The eggs are heavier than water and will stay on the bottom. After fertilizing them, the male will linger, gently fanning the eggs with his tail, washing water over them, making sure that the eggs are clean and in no danger of being suffocated. The eggs hatch and the small fry emerge, and they begin to feed on small bits, freshwater crabs, midge nymphs, and, when they get larger, on the nymphs of mayflies, caddis flies, and stone flies, not to mention anything else that happens to fall into the stream. The fish grow and move into deep pools (where the current isn't so strong and where it takes less work to stay head upstream) and become larger, forming those spots on their sides. They are a sensitive fish, and I am convicted that they can feel in the water the vibration of men approaching (this is certainly correct when the water is low in August or early September). I like to sit where I can watch their sides flashing when they feed on the bottom, and I take pleasure in them, in their presence, the gift they bring to ponds and streams, and I know at these times what dullness there would be to water without them. There are moments when I try to see them and can't and for one horrifying second I believe they have gone for good. Then I will hear the plop or see the dimple made by a rising fish. When I sit on the banks in the evenings of June or July, I take faith in the brook trout's single-mindedness of purpose, one so profound as to lack (or need) anything like awareness. . . .

Now, after writing this, I went fishing in the evenings, and I could think about, or at least see, the rest of the book. I went to work in earnest. It wasn't long before I sent some of it to New York.

5

Most jobs have jokes that almost always reveal some secret that only the initiated know. For screenwriters (a little of which work I have done) the joke is this: There was a starlet who was so stupid she tried to do herself some good by sleeping with the screenwriter of a movie. As everyone in the business knows, the screenwriter is a long way down the food chain from, say, the producer. And then there is the story about a writer who comes home and finds that his neighbors have been killed, that the carpenters who were working on his house have been shot, too. There are bodies everywhere. The writer finds both uniform cops and detectives in his backyard. They look at the devastation. The writer says, "What happened?" The police say, "We don't know. All we know is that this happened just after your agent called." "My agent called?" said the writer. "My god, what did he say?"

My agent did call. This was a generous, energetic, and intelligent man. One of the difficulties in the writing life is that you have to learn that a large part of the work is not between you and the book you are writing but also between you and the people who publish it and represent you. My experience is that these are people who are under enormous pressure, and that this should never be forgotten. When you work alone, it is easy to think you are more important than you are. Learning to handle pressure is a large part of the writing life, and because I didn't know this years ago, I misunderstood this man, the agent who called, and of course, I am sorry to have made the mistakes I did with him and that we ended up going our separate ways. Who isn't sorry for an error of understanding? Or for the fact that often, when you do understand, it is too late?

Now, though, the gloom lifted. Everything was fine. A man by the name of Sam Lawrence believed in the book and advanced me enough money so that I could finish it.

"Just like I always said," said Christina.

"Uh-huh," I said.

"What's a little anxiety between friends, anyway?" she said. "Are you going to go down to the Mongaup tonight?"

"For a little bit," I said. When I caught a brook trout, I held it for a moment before letting it go, and as I did, I thought, "Thank god. You really saved me that time."

We spent the winter there in that small green house, and one more, and then it was time to go—what we had gotten from the land was over. The house was too small for the three of us, and the isolation had gotten tough. We packed and moved to Vermont.

We moved to a house in the mountains, or at least, they were mountains by eastern standards. I thought they were hills, by the yardstick that I had grown up with in the West, which is to say by the standards of the Sierras or the Rockies. That didn't make the winters any easier, and in the middle of the first one, we had to go upstairs to look out the window, because the drifts were so deep.

In the spring, my wife said, "I think it's time for you to show Abbey how to catch a fish. A brook trout."

In the woods behind the house there was a stream, not so much different, really, from Fish Cabin. It was surrounded by softwoods, although it didn't pool up in the same way, and this stream was surrounded by jewelweed, which was now in bloom. Abbey was three years old. Christina looked at me with a searching glance, not a challenge exactly, but with a certain intensity of expectation. I had Abbey on my knee, and I said, "Sure."

We went out the door of the house and turned toward the woods. Here there was a path that was lined with azaleas, now in bloom, and we went along, the three of us, my daughter in the middle, me with a fly rod. Now, as anyone knows, trying to catch a fish on cue, on demand, is a perilous activity. Of course, I could use the standard explanations, such as it is too hot or too cold or too early or too late. Too much water or too little. God knows, I have used them all at one time or another. Still, we went through the jewelweed, the orange and green cascade seeming cheerful but fraught with the possibilities of failure. We stepped into the shade of the trees, where we heard the sound of running water. It was that time in Vermont that doesn't last long: between snowmelt and blackflies. It was a clear day, and there were hawks in the air, over the field.

"Hawks are out," I said.

"Uh-huh," said Christina. "It's shady back in there by the brook."

"Well, I was just pointing out the hawks. That's all."

"What do hawks have to do with it?" said Abbey.

We crawled in behind a rock, on the upstream side of a pool, where I was willing to bet there were some good-sized brook trout. My daughter waited.

On the first cast, a brook trout took the fly, a Hare's Ear, with—or so it seems to me—all the urgency of a promise being kept. Frankly, I am not sure who was more surprised, the fish or me. I lifted it from the stream: a big one, too, sparkling there in my hand. Christina and Abbey made a sound of sweet surprise. I let the trout go. Christina blushed with pleasure at the moment, and then we turned back to the house. Whatever our problems had been were gone, the disappearance of them somehow validated by the promise of the brook trout.

As we went back to the house and as Abbey ran ahead, screaming brook trout! brook trout! Christina said, "You know, I think we should have another child."

Three

I

Tatie, our second daughter, was born in the middle of an easy winter that turned into a hard, snowy spring. Where we lived in Vermont that year there was snow on the ground in late May. But we had the new baby, who, along with her sister, proved that it is not what parents give to children that is obvious or striking, but the reverse. The real treat was what the children gave to us. A few years ago, Tatie asked me to come out and play with her, and when I resisted, she said, "Come on, Dad, these are memories." She was right, of course—I didn't know then that some of the most inconceivably important things seem, at the time, so ordinary. For instance, one winter Tatie and I tried to build an igloo in front of the house, making blocks by packing a plastic box with snow and then dumping each one out, like white bricks.

At about the time Tatie was born, I started looking for beaver ponds. The pleasure in fishing them, or the ones I was looking for anyway, was not only that they were filled with brook trout, but that they were a good distance from a road. And the way I went about picking them was on the basis of how far away from a road they were. The farther the better. I remember reading some place that there is no location in the continental United States, or at least the lower forty-eight states, that is more than ten miles from a road, not necessarily a paved one, but a road nevertheless. I am not sure if this is true, but I can say that I sure tried to put it to the test in Vermont.

Anticipation at a certain time of the year is almost as good as taking the first step into a stream, or as pleasurable as seeing a ring spreading at the head of a pool where an insect, a Hendrickson, say, has just disappeared. Still, there are times when anticipation comes to something less than one had hoped, and my favorite story about this was told to me by a friend. When he was a boy, his father had planned a fishing trip for the two of them to the Upper Peninsula in Michigan, and one of the aspects of this trip that got the boy most excited was the fact that they were going to have an Indian guide. Or, as my friend put it, a "real" Indian guide. For weeks before this trip took place, my friend badgered his father every night about whether or not there was going to be a real Indian guide. Did his father promise? The critical thing my friend was concerned about was the method by which the guide would start a fire. He assumed that the guide would get out a bow and a piece of hard wood and some shavings and that the guide would use these things to get a fire going. My friend dreamed about this moment. Finally, the day came. They went to Michigan and were met on the shore of a lake by the guide, who was an Indian. He had a boat with an outboard engine, and he took my friend and the friend's father across the lake. There the guide set up camp. He made a fire. My friend watched as the guide piled up some driftwood, poured a gallon of gas on it, and touched it off with a match, thrown in from a safe distance. The explosion knocked everyone flat. "And let me tell you, that sucker burned," my friend said, his eyes set on the horizon when he told me this part. He shrugged. What can you do about things that don't work out the way you wanted?

But it can work the other way, too. I usually started with a U.S. Geological Survey map, which I bought and pored over in the middle of winter, looking for damp places a long way from everything, and then in the spring, or what would be early summer in other places, I got ready to go fishing.

One of the pleasures of fishing is anticipation of it, and these winter nights were an exercise in imagination perfectly imbued with a sense of practicality. Even now I can remember the smell of a new map; the sound the rubber band made as I took it off the tube of paper; the small rattle, almost thunderlike, as I spread the sheet out on the dining room table. I got out a square and sharpened a pencil, the scent of it a little bitter, and then I drew lines of declension across the beaver meadows, the contours, the blue rills of streams, and the green sections that showed the out-of-the-way timber. Given how far I was walking to get to these ponds, the difference between true north and magnetic north had to be taken into consideration if I wanted to come out at the place where I had left my car. The yellow light overhead washed down, leaving me with the metal square, bent over the map, making long lines with the tip of a newly sharpened pencil.

I took out my fly boxes and put the teakettle on the stove, and when a plume of steam was coming out of the spout, I stuck the barb of a fly into the eraser of a pencil and then used this to hold the fly in the steam. The hackles, the wings straightened out, just like new. I'd tie some Royal Wulffs on a #16 hook, just in case I found some new, fast water, and then I'd take a small lunch, a fly rod, the flies, a leader pouch, the map, an orienteering compass, and I'd start walking. Part of the fun of this fishing was the notion that I had to be careful, and that if I fell down and got hurt, a long ways from a road, why, then it would be a very bad moment. The alertness this possibility brought to the operation made everything seem brighter than usual, and, if anything, the land I walked across and the ponds I found under these circumstances seemed a little more real.

I liked to find a dam that had only been in existence for a year or two. This seemed to make for good fishing, because, or so it seemed to me, the fishing is best in a beaver pond that hasn't been around for too long. I think this is because in the beginning, right after the dam has been built, the trout don't have to fight the current anymore and the insect populations are good, so the trout get fat. Then something happens to the bottom of the pond. Maybe the accumulation of debris kills the mayfly nymphs and caddis larva and the insect population just about disappears, but whatever the reason, the fishing seems to drop off after the first couple of years.

There was one pond I liked, and it took about an hour and a half to walk to it from the road. The place where I parked my car was not far from what was left of a town that had been beaten down by the winters to the extent that some of the buildings had fallen in. A barn looked as though a bomb had gone off inside, blowing everything straight up, and the beams and siding, the gray shingles had all fallen straight back down and ended up in a heap. Even in late spring you could feel an eddy of winter, an arctic promise that surely had been kept.

I used to start walking where a stream went under the road. A trail began there, but it only went a half mile or so, and then it petered out near a pond that most people thought was out of the way, but which, by the rules of engagement that I was using, was just the beginning. After the trail disappeared, it was a matter of going around the brush, or working my way through the woods, where the going was easier. At the top of the Green Mountain

National Forest, the land flattened out, and in the meadows there were beaver ponds. I stood on the dam of one I liked, feeling the spongy quality of it beneath my feet, and cast as far into the pond as I could, retrieving the fly, a wet or a nymph fished like a wet, until I felt that tug. If I hit it right, these places were stiff with brookies.

All was not perfect on these expeditions. One day I was standing on this dam, retrieving a fly slowly, letting it sink, and then giving it a little jerk or lifting the tip of the rod to make it rise, and then letting it sink again. In my mind I was trying to suggest the anxiety of a living thing in a place where it can get eaten, and as I was concentrating on the movement of the fly and imagining it underwater, I didn't see a beaver that was swimming across the pond, from my right to left, or, to put it another way, toward the fly line. This is one of those moments where there is nothing to do. I was afraid that if I started stripping in, the hook would catch the beaver, and I guessed that my only chance was to wait until it swam over the line, but of course the beaver was too intent on some other purpose, angling not toward the line, but the leader, and then not toward just the leader, but the fly. I thought I could break him off (surely, the stuff of ignominy, breaking off a beaver) if I hooked him, and so I thought maybe I should strip the line in, but as I took the first length of it, the beaver managed to wrap itself into the heavy part of the leader. So there I was, fast to a forty-pound beaver. And immediately I thought, Yes, this is the time some friends are going to show up and say, "So, that's how you do it? I always wondered."

It took a little while, but I managed to cut the beaver loose, although there were a couple of close calls with its teeth. This is the kind of small thing that often goes wrong in fishing, like having a bat take a fly when you are false casting just at dusk. And while I was embarrassed by the notion of having a friend see me in moments like this, the truth is that at these times it is probably a good idea to have a friend around, no matter what the immediate cost in embarrassment, if only to have someone to be able to validate otherwise unbelievable stories.

2

I know of a fisherman—not me, thank god—who used to take his dog with him when he went to a stream not far from where I live. One day this guy managed to hook his dog on the backcast, and the dog took off through the woods, stripping out the entire fly line and getting into the backing.

And then, once, a fisherman of my acquaintance was wading a stream in central Vermont. A road ran next to the stream, and an ambulance driving along it got into an accident just above the place where my friend was fishing. While the ambulance driver waited for a tow truck and the police to arrive, he put a cooler into the stream, since it was a hot day, and he was taking an organ from one hospital to another for a transplant. The organ was packed in ice, but the driver wanted to make sure that it was going to stay cool. All my friend saw was the cooler, which had gotten away from the driver and was floating in the stream. Now, there is no need to go into just what it was that was inside the cooler, but it wasn't the kind of thing you would expect to find when you go fishing in Vermont. A friend is always good to have when the unexpected comes along.

At about this time (when I was looking for out-of-the-way beaver ponds), I received a letter that scared me pretty bad. It was a threatening letter, and while anyone who publishes books gets some odd mail, this was different. I don't know how to explain the difference between this and the usually odd mail, aside from saying that the instant I received this letter, I knew something was wrong. It had been mailed locally, and it was long, detailed, and had a kind of pathological stink to it. This was not the work of anyone who could be dismissed as a crank, or as a nuisance, since the details it invoked in its threats were too stark. Also, it came not long after a woman had been murdered in a town close to the one where I live, and the murderer had never been caught. The murder had been a random event, and it seemed to be just as anonymous as it had been brutal. The anonymous quality of the murder seemed to blend perfectly with the letter I received. The letter told me that if I wanted to go on living, I should play along. I would have to pay some money.

The odd thing about making friends is that you often find them in unexpected circumstances. The FBI agent I met in a parking lot, not long after I received this letter, became a friend. I'll call him Bill. We met in a parking lot because he didn't want to come to my house, in case the place was being watched. This possibility didn't make me feel great, but I was glad that he had thought of it. The parking lot we met in was close to the Williams River, which I used to fish from time to time. It was a spring day, and rags of clouds, gray underneath, fluffy on top, dragged along in the sky.

I got into the FBI agent's car and showed him the letter. He was in his early thirties, and I found out later that he had been a lawyer, but he had grown tired of divorce work and real estate closings, just as he had felt ill at ease with the notion of the law being used to conceal rather than to expose. He had dark hair, dark eyes, and he was wearing a dark suit and a tie.

"What do you think?" I said.

"I don't know," he said. "It doesn't look too good."

"No," I said. "You know there was a woman killed close by." I told him the name of the town.

"I'm aware of that," he said. "We're aware of that."

The letter wanted me to communicate with the writer of it, who called himself Jasper, and the way I was supposed to do it was through the local paper, which ran a series of small, boxed ads on the front page. If I was willing to cooperate, I was supposed to put an ad in the paper. Jasper was going to ask me for something.

"We'd like to catch this guy," said Bill. "I guess we'll put an ad in the paper."

"No," I said. "If you go down to the paper and put in an ad, it will get around pretty fast that the FBI is up to something, and this is a small town. The guy told me not to go to the police. I'll go down and do it."

"I guess that's right," said Bill. "Do you have someplace where you can send your kids?"

"Boston," I said.

"I think it would be a good idea if they went there," he said. "Until this is over."

Bill gave me a device to put on my phone, which allowed me to record a call, if Jasper should call. Bill also sent the letter to a man I like to think of as Mycroft Holmes, who, of course, was Sherlock's smarter brother. This Mycroft's job was to read letters like this one, and to make an estimate, based on years of experience, of just what its author was likely to do. Jasper left no doubt about what would happen if it got out that I had gone to the police. Or, at least, he gave me something to think about along these lines.

Of course, one of the difficulties of moments like these is what can only be called the reality factor. Everything is vague and uncertain, and it is hard to know what is really happening: Is this a letter that should be ignored, or is there something behind it? Are you in danger or aren't you? And, if you try to catch someone like this, if only to get him out of your life, have you made something that was previously just an illusion (a threat) into something that had become, by your actions, quite real?

"What do you think we should do?" said Christina.

"I'm not sure," I said. I thought for a moment of what it would be like to live in our house, waiting, listening at night if we just ignored the threats.

"What happens if we start playing with this guy and they don't catch him, what then?" she said. "Oh, God."

"What are we going to do, move?" I said. "Are we just going to pull up stakes and clear out? And what about that woman, the one who got murdered?"

We sat in the kitchen, the golden light of it falling over us. My waders and fly rod were in the corner by the door.

"I guess we'd better take the kids to Boston," she said.

On the weekend, Bill came to the house, driving his own car, a Jeep, and wearing blue jeans and a flannel shirt. He looked around the house and said, "There's no lock on the front door."

"We haven't needed one," I said. "Who would bother us out here?"

"You should get a lock for the door," said Bill. We nailed some of the windows shut, the ones without locks on them, and the door in my office, which is in the attic, and opens on to the hillside behind the house.

I put the ad in the paper to say I was willing to cooperate. Then I sat down to wait, or, I should say, Christina and I sat down to wait. With the kids away, the house was quiet. It is a large house, a place with white siding and green shutters, that is just the thing people have in mind when they think they'd like to give it all up and move to the country to write a novel, but they haven't tried heating it or coming to terms with the frozen pipes when it gets to be thirty-five below zero.

Another letter came from Jasper. It told me to get some flashing—the kind of thing you use on the roof around the chimney—some tape, some white paint, and a pair of waders. Fishing waders. Also, some money. When I had these things, I was supposed to put another ad in the paper to say I was ready. My notion was that this guy had an idea of me wading across a stream to drop off the "money," and I even wondered if it would be water that I had fished.

There is always something cheerful about a tackle store in the springtime, when people pick over the flies and look at new fly rods, wondering if they should buy one. Hope and anticipation is

56

so thick at these times that you can feel it, like a breeze. It was pleasant to feel it when I bought a new pair of waders.

Bill came by from time to time, and we talked about fishing. He had never been, but he wanted to go. One day, he spent some time looking through Caucci's and Nastasi's *Hatches*. He had also read a book of mine, in which brook trout were described. We liked a lot of the same writers, and Bill told me that while he had been on a stakeout, he had read a book of a friend of mine.

I put another ad in the paper. I said I had the things and was ready. Bill told me that Mycroft Holmes had said that he thought Jasper was a smart guy and that he would be very hard to catch, and that one of the things that Jasper was afraid of was being exposed. The thing I recall, though, is the nights while Christina and I waited for the next letter. I lay awake, looking into the dark. The atmosphere in the room, each small noise, any ticking or natural sound, all seemed filled with the possibility of malice. I thought that if I could, I would love to get into the mountains, up to a beaver dam, to stand there and make long casts across the pond. I could imagine it perfectly, clouds reflected in the surface, which was dimpled with rising trout, so as to look like they were in the clouds.

"Why did we start this anyway?" said Christina. "We should have just ignored the entire thing. Look. Just look at what's happening to us."

At the foot of the bed there was a table with a shotgun on it and a box of shells. We had a drill that we went through if I had to go downstairs in the middle of the night to look into the cause of a sound. This was a procedure to guarantee that I wouldn't make a mistake: Who knew what could happen if Christina started wandering around, too, when I was downstairs with a shotgun? She was to stay in the bedroom, no matter what.

When we went to Boston, we drove the way Bill had taught us. For instance, we were supposed to turn into a cul-de-sac and to wait there to see if we were being followed. Never take the exact same route twice.

Another letter came. It said that I should wrap up the money in the flashing, tape it, paint it white, and be ready to drop it off. The waders, the letter said, were "to walk through the blood in your house if you betray me."

"What kind of asshole would say things like that?" said Christina. "Goddamn it. They better catch this guy."

Later, in the dark, my wife said, "What are you thinking about?"

"A beaver pond," I said. "In the Green Mountains."

3

On one of those weekends when we were going to go down to Boston to see our kids, an exterminator was going to come to the house. Bill always wanted to know who was going to be coming to the house, and so before leaving I told him that the exterminator was going to show up. We were going to have to leave early, to get to Boston, and the exterminator said he would be at our house at 5:30 in the morning. Bill thought about this, and on the day we were supposed to leave, he was there, at 5:30, just to make sure everything was all right. Then we stood in the driveway and laughed. The *exterminator?* Well, it's moments like that when you realize that you are making a friend.

The next letter came. It said that there was an abandoned mailbox in a river town in New Hampshire, and that I should make a package filled with money and drive it to the abandoned mailbox at ten in the morning. Then I should come back at ten at night, and if the package was still there, I should bring it home and in the morning I should take it back at ten, and then check again at ten at night to see if it was still there. I should keep doing this until the package was gone.

The FBI made a package that had a radio transmitter inside. At this point, it seemed that it would be a good idea for Christina to go to Boston to be with our kids. On the morning that I was supposed to drop off the package, Bill came over with a bullet-proof vest, in plastic from the dry cleaner. It was white, with Velcro straps on the sides, and for a moment I wondered who usually wore it? Mob informants? The Velcro straps on the side were to make it fit snugly. The sound of those Velcro straps seemed familiar. It was the sound that the flaps of my fly vest made when I opened one to take out a fly box.

Bill put a shotgun in the back seat of my car. We drove to the abandoned mailbox. In the bushes around it there were four or five men, in camouflage, all of them well armed with automatic weapons. Bill and I went back to my house to wait until ten at night.

What had occurred to both of us is that perhaps the writer of the letters wasn't thinking about picking the "money" up at the mailbox, but that he would be waiting for me at my house when I returned with the package in the evening. Bill put a .38 pistol in the magazine rack in the bathroom, and he told me that if we came back to the house and that the writer of the letters was inside, I was to do whatever I could to get into the bathroom, make any excuse, and to come out with the pistol. Bill looked through *Hatches* as we waited. We talked about the difference between fishing a fly upstream and down.

It got dark. It was time to go back to the mailbox, but on our way there Bill was told (by radio) that the FBI had caught two guys, who had shown up and tried to take the package.

Their story was this: One of them had received a phone call that afternoon from a man who said, "You don't remember me, but a long time ago, you did me a favor. I want to pay you back. If you go to a mailbox, across the river in New Hampshire, there's something for you in it." The caller said he would check in later to see if it had worked out.

Now, I'm not sure how the FBI agents who had been in the brush all day took this, but surely it was with a certain amount of skepticism. However, to be on the safe side, they went to the apartment of the man, whom I'll call Jim, who had received this call. They put a tape machine on his phone.

At eleven o'clock, Jim's phone rang. The caller asked if Jim had picked up the package. Jim was both angry that he had gotten into this mess and he was still scared about having been arrested by a bunch of guys in camouflage who were carrying machine guns. He said, "Yeah. It's filled with money."

The caller sent a letter to Jim about a week later. In it he said that Jim should take the package out to a back road and bury it. Now, this is the last thing in the world the FBI wanted, since this meant that they would have to watch the place where the money was buried, and, of course, the money could be left there for years. All they could do was to have Jim put an ad on the front page of the paper in which he said that he didn't want the money, didn't want to play around anymore, that he was tired of the entire thing and that he was going to stick the "money" back in the mailbox where he had first picked it up.

The agents waited on the day the money was supposed to be back in the mailbox. But the man who had written letters to me, and who had called Jim, just disappeared. Just like that.

"So, they didn't catch him? *Great*," said Christina. "Now what? Can you tell me? He knows we went to the police. He's got to.

61

And so now we have put him in the position of making good on his threat. Great."

The worst part, I discovered, about an experience like this is that it poisons the well of one's associations. You begin to wonder if people you know were the ones who were up to such a trick as this. What about those people who were having financial trouble? Did you ever say something that was misunderstood or that could conceivably be perceived as unfriendly? Every now and then, in the middle of the night, an old house like this will make a noise.

It took a while, but it was obvious that the only thing to do was to start going back to the beaver ponds. I'd take a lunch and go, or at least, I would when Christina and the children were in Boston or out doing something, because I didn't want to be away from the house if they were there. I'd walk for hours, glad to know that I would be able to stand on one of those spongy dams, casting into that tea-colored water, watching the surface of it, which was dimpled with fish.

Four

I

*W*hen my older daughter was twelve, I began to teach her to do some fly fishing. Mostly, of course, I have been safe on trout streams, but when it comes to teaching something to a child, you are aware that there are certain parts that, while not obviously dangerous, don't reveal their secrets until you've had a scare. I often think that it is a father's job to try to anticipate as many of these moments as you can, although there comes a time when you have to let go. Still, when it came to teaching my daughter something about catching trout—brook and others—there were some difficulties I wanted to make clear.

Some years ago I was fishing on the White River, which is one of Vermont's larger streams. The water was high, but I was still wading, and while I knew that one should never wade downstream in heavy water, somehow I disregarded this rule. I stepped into the head of a deep pool. I went down far enough for the water to come up to my chest and even to come over the tops of my waders. I turned around and faced upstream and immediately saw my predicament: I could not go back the way I had come because the weight of the current was too great, and yet downstream the water was even deeper, over my head. There was nothing to do but swim for it, keeping an eye on the boulders that stuck out of the greenish water of spring. So, I wanted to be careful about what I told my daughter, especially when it came to hidden danger.

We began with casting, starting out on the lawn with a bit of yarn instead of a fly, and even when we went to a pond up the road and I tied on a Royal Coachman, I broke off the sharp part of the hook. It didn't take long before she could handle a fair amount of line. We talked about wading. Insects. How the water moves in a stream and how the trout use the current, and that they often will find a place at a seam between fast water and slow. In the winter, I started to show her how to tie flies. During one of these times, she said, "What's it like to be in love?"

She said this with the same frankness she might have used in asking when white mayflies appear on the water. Mostly, she was not too interested in tying flies, but often what one learns takes years to have an effect or even a use. I didn't make a big deal about trying to teach her, since this would work out in its own way. I showed her some flies I'd tied and sometimes she'd watch when I got ready to tie a pattern. She asked about being in love when I was getting ready to tie some Hendricksons.

One of the things about tying flies is that you can adjust the patterns so as to reflect the slight variations in the species found on the water that you fish. The Hendricksons on the water that I fish a lot have gray glassine wings, which remind me of silk stockings, and their bodies have a little pink in them, the same color as the vernal blush the trees have just before they begin to put out leaves. To get this color into the pattern I mix in a little pink fur with the imitation fox I use to make the body. I buy some Australian possum, and I dye a piece of it in a pot on the stove. I was cooking the fur when she asked about love.

For a moment we looked at each other through the pink mist that rose from the pot. The sensation of being a "father" was so keen I felt it on my face like a mask, but if there was a mask there, I wanted to drop it and be absolutely direct.

"There are all kinds of love," I said.

"Like what kinds?" she said.

"Well, you could be passionately in love," I said.

She looked at me, considering this. I immediately thought about how much, if at all, we should talk about AIDS. We had talked about it before. Now, though, it seemed best not to harp on it like some anxiety-stricken creature.

"Then there are other kinds of love, too. You can love a friend. You can be married to someone for fifty years, and what you feel then might be different, even stronger than what you felt when you were first courting. There are all kinds."

This sounded a lot like a counter on which endless varieties of love were displayed, like bolts of cloth, but I was stuck with it.

"Which kind is the best?" she said.

I looked into the pot, where the roiling surface was marked with foam. The only way to get the fur out was to reach in with a long fork. The dye ran off it, and we listened as it dripped back into the pot, the sound seeming to be a perfect combination of memories (on my part) and anticipation (on her part).

"That's hard to say," I said. "What do you think?"

"How would I know?" she said.

She stared right at me.

"Well?" she said. "I want to know the truth."

"It varies with how old you are," I said. "I like the kind that really lasts. But I guess you have to decide for yourself which you like best."

She looked at the wet fur.

"What are you going to tie?" she said.

"Some Hendricksons," I said.

"Oh," she said. "We'll go fishing in the spring, won't we?"

"Sure," I said. "Yes. Of course. Yes. My darling."

2

But the discussion of love had somehow gotten mixed up in my mind with catching trout, and particularly brook trout (which are found in wild places), and this combination left me with a lot of questions. What was it I was really trying to convey to my daughter by teaching her the habits of mayflies, the times of their emergence, or how you recognize each variety of trout? This question is made concrete for me when I think of a piece of water I fish whenever I get a chance.

It is about an hour's drive from where I live and one of the things I like best about it is that it flows through a valley filled with farms that have been there for a long time and the landscape, aside from an occasional new barn or a new tractor, looks the way it did a hundred years ago. I like to fish a long pool, deep along the bank, and at the head of it there is a run where the water passes over some gravel or rubble. An apple tree grows on the bank, and in the spring, when the Hendricksons are on the water, the flowers of the tree are reflected on the surface of the glide. The fish rise to the mayflies, dimpling the water and sometimes making a splash, the trout showing themselves in an explosion of water as they fall back into the stream. Of course, some of the most fun to be had here is in the anticipation after you cast the fly a few feet above the dimple. Mostly, waiting is an unpleasant proposition, but not here.

On these spring afternoons, when I stand in this spot, I try to forget my worries as much as possible, and for a while, when the fish are rising, it seems that I exist outside time, although in the midst of all this, I will have a memory of some kind, a bit of piercing intimacy. It is not that I am peaceful at this moment so much as comfortably alive and excited, although I feel something like humility, too. I think about my dead father. Maybe I will consider the time he tried to get those four saplings to grow into the shape of a chair. I am alone, but not lonely at all.

This moment, I guess, is what I want to convey to my daughter. But how much of this will she take as her own, and will she understand that this was the thing I was trying not to teach but to give?

The fish I usually catch here are rainbows, wild fish, bright red on the sides, a little green on the back and with some spots, although from time to time I will catch some brook trout here, too. The river valley is small, and on each side of it there are some hills of irregular shape, some of them bare and showing gray rock. I let the fish go, carefully putting them back, since the pleasure has long since turned into catching them rather than eating them. I would like to think that one day my daughter might stand in this same spot and remember, as she makes her casts, those winter nights when we dyed fur and talked about love. She'll have her own memories by then, and, with any luck, in a moment of keen distraction, she'll see the rainbows and brook trout rising along the bank.

Five

I

I have always been interested in the places where you can find brook trout, and I took a job that let me spend some time flying with bush pilots in Maine. I had always been fascinated with men who made a living this way and, of course, some of the best brook trout water in the country is in Maine. I flew with a number of pilots—Scott Skinner, Gary Dumond, Dick Fulsome—all of them having that same air of a man who is applying abstract principles to exceedingly practical circumstances. For instance, they told me that the problem of landing on a pond was that the water was never the same twice, and what might have been all right one day could have a log floating in it the next. Dick Fulsome told me about how when the weather was bad, he came home on the "iron beam," by which he meant when there were too many clouds or too much fog to see, he found a railroad track and followed it home. "You've got to pick your lines, though. You don't want one with a tunnel on it. And you've got to stay to the right, in case someone else is doing the same thing in the other direction."

I also met a man by the name of Jack McPhee. He had been a warden pilot for twenty-five years, and then had retired to run a lodge for fishermen and hunters. In addition to the lodge, he had a cabin on an isolated pond. Jack was of medium height, smart and calm, funny in many ways, slow to anger, but once angry it was a good idea to stay away from him. He had blue eyes and dark hair. When I went to spend time with bush pilots, Jack and I talked about what can go wrong when flying an airplane, and one of the things I asked about was a fire. I will never forget his voice, one that had been refined for years so as to deal with tension, or with trouble. He looked at me and said, in the precise voice necessary to respond to such a circumstance, "An onboard fire is a major emergency."

When I was about to leave, Jack said to me that I should come back to go fishing sometime. He told me that he had spent a lot of time when he was a warden pilot looking down at ponds in out-of-the-way places. He bet I'd like to fish a couple of them. Would I like to go sometime?

I remember flying over one of these ponds with another warden pilot, who looked down at the tea-colored water and said,

"Well, if you ever want to catch some brook trout as big as your arm, that's the place to do it."

2

It took a couple of years, but I kept thinking about those tea-colored ponds, and when I decided to go back, all I had was a telephone number. When I called Jack, I discovered this was a radio phone. In Jack's part of the world there are no telephones, and using a radio phone is like using a radio, which means you cannot hear the person you are speaking to when you are talking. When you are done, you say "Over." Jack still had a cabin on an isolated pond. No other buildings on it, and I was welcome to it. A few days later I received a note from Jack's wife, who wrote "Jack says to bring some Hornbergs and weighted Woolly Buggers."

Right from the beginning, even in the preparations to get away, there was some tantalizing ingredient, some promise of questions to be answered. It seemed that right on the edge of awareness, just in the shadows, or in the only half-acknowledged consciousness, there was something stirring. Certainly, I wanted to get away, and Christina did, too. In another age, I would have admitted to a spiritual fatigue, but this was only part of it: Beneath it all there lurked a submerged, chaotic impulse. What came to mind, as I began to pack, was a line I had read in Camus's notebook, an entry that isn't even a sentence, but which runs, "That wild longing for clarity."

It ran through my mind as I contemplated the things I spread out on and around the dining-room table: food, bedding, clothes, fly rods, shoes, rain gear, a six-pack of beer, a device known as a "sun shower," a filter to pump drinking water from the pond, books . . . I had been wanting to read Emerson's essays for years, particularly "Experience" and "Nature." Christina was more practically minded: She likes pasta with shrimp, and she was experimenting with frozen jumbos and dry ice, which made a whitish mist in the cooler she packed. The mist had a cold, acrid scent of the arctic, which reminded me of those trout ponds in Maine in the depths of winter, their secrets locked up until spring. Well, with a spiritual chill that came from shoving aside those unanswered longings, I contemplated the first hard fact. Small airplanes can't lift much weight. Everything we were going to take, frozen shrimp included, must weigh less than two hundred and fifty pounds.

Abbey, who was then fifteen, began to weigh the packages. She carried them into the bathroom, got on the scale, then subtracted her weight.

Jack McPhee's plane wasn't big enough to carry Christina and me and our things to the pond I wanted to go to, so I contacted Central Maine Flying, which agreed to send a plane to a lake nearby in New Hampshire, where we would meet it. Now, though, we looked at the things we had packed. My wife called the flying service. I had been sculling all summer and was down to a hundred and sixty-five pounds. The flying service allowed us a little more weight.

Christina's parents have a house at Squam Lake, and we met the plane there. We loaded our boxes and bags, a fly rod, and waved good-bye to our children, who were staying with their grandparents. The pilot taxied into the middle of the lake. What excitement can compare with the moment when a pilot, in a small plane, turns into the wind and opens the throttle?

My wife sat up front, and I got into the back, looking over the seats at the instrument panel. The dials, the white letters on black backgrounds, the digital display of the flight clock of the navigational equipment all suggested precision: Here, at least you could tell what was really going on.

As we turned north, I thought of a story that a friend, Howard Mosher, told me. Like all fishing stories, it is about the difference between appearance and reality. Howard's son, Jake, went fishing in the springtime, and Jake's favorite hole is on a stream that runs through a farm in northern Vermont. Jake is a friendly, polite young man, and as he fished the hole, he talked to the farmer who owned the land the stream ran through. Jake noticed, as they talked, that his sunken leader had begun to move. He lifted the tip of the fly rod and felt the sure, definite tug of an enormous fish. It sulked on the bottom, the way a large brown trout will. Jake fought this thing for a half hour, never seeing more than an enormous dark swirl in the depths. As a joke, he said to the farmer, "Maybe we should shoot this thing."

The farmer turned and ran to the house. He came back with a shotgun.

"For god's sake, don't shoot the leader," said Jake.

The shotgun went off, and a crown-shaped splash appeared in the water. Jake's ears started to ring. The fish was still fighting. The farmer said, "I can't take any more of this."

The farmer climbed down into the pool with a net he had brought from his house. He jabbed it here and there into the dark swirls. "God, Oh, god," he said. "That is not a fish. It's a snapping turtle. Got to weigh fifty pounds."

Now, we lost altitude. The altimeter spun backward like a clock in a dream, and down below, the earth seemed less remote. The land was northern forest, a mixture of softwoods—such as spruce and pine—and hardwoods, like oak. Here and there I saw the S-shaped and silver meandering of a river. We flew along the shore of the pond where we were going, and as we made a turn, the g-forces pulled on my face. Down below the trees streaked by, then we turned and landed on the surface of the pond.

We unloaded at a makeshift dock below the cabin. The pilot said he would come back in a week, and then he slammed the door, started the engine, and taxied away, the sound of the engine increasing as he took off, water trailing from the pontoons.

The pond was about forty acres. The cabin was made of logs with a pitched roof and a porch. Copper tubing ran along the interior log walls, and here and there a small gas lamp was attached to it. Each lamp had a small shade in which there was an ashy mantle, delicate as a memory.

I cooked shrimp pasta, browning a little garlic and discarding it, cooking the shrimp quickly until they were tender, almost translucent. It was evening when I cooked, and the lights in the cabin were on. They made a quiet noise, a kind of throaty hiss, and they gave off a familiar light. Outside, on the pond, loons cried.

Christina turned to listen. What I remembered was that time in New York City, before we had gone to that green house, when she had put her hands together and made that sound. As we sat in the cabin on the isolated pond in Maine (filled with brook trout), the pasta cooking, the scent of garlic in the air, the sound of loons reverberated back to that apartment in New York.

When the sun was up I took a walk. Blue damselflies were in the air, like needles of turquoise, their wings nothing more than filaments, and around them there were orange butterflies. Beyond them raspberries hung ruby-like in the shade. I saw blueberries, too, the end of each having a small shape like a crown. The accumulation of insects, the quick paths they described in the air (like the random path of memory or desire), the jeweled colors in the undergrowth, the sudden liveliness made me confront what I was looking for, and why I came to the places where brook trout exist.

There is nothing vague about these places. They have no use for lies. On the far shore of the pond, in the stands of trees, in the insects, in the presence of brook trout there was nothing devious. Nothing threatening. As I turned back to the cabin, I thought of the Emerson I read the night before. He said that there were times in the woods when he had been "glad to the brink of fear."

Of course, I wanted to take some of this home, but I was not sure how to do it. As I walked back to the cabin it seemed that what was so strong here existed in other places, too, and I had felt it at other times, even in New York City and in Boston, when my children were born, their heads crowning into the world, their arms and legs jerking with the shock of birth. Well, yes, "glad to the point of fear."

3

Later I heard the sound of a small airplane, a Super Piper. It was distant at first, but it got louder in a minute, at once practical and reassuring—in the whine of an aviation engine, there is something of the tractor. The plane came up to the dock, and Jack McPhee got out. He stood on the dock, wearing a pair of pants with suspenders and a well-washed plaid shirt. One hand reached out to hold the wing of the airplane as we talked.

We flew into a pond that was about twenty miles away, tied up the plane, and went into the woods. The place where we were going was one of those Jack had seen in his days as a warden pilot. It was too small to fly into directly, and the only way to get there was to fly to the closest body of water and then to start walking. It is hard to imagine a place that is more isolated. We went through a cedar bog, and Jack pointed out to Christina the flowers that grew here and there: a rattlesnake orchid, Indian pipes. The path we walked on was not well defined, and, in fact, it was hard to call it a path at all. The brush was damp, and we got wet from the waist down.

The pond was small, about twenty acres or so, and in the middle there was an island of half an acre. It was still early and there was no wind. The reflection of trees and sky, of the island, had the aspect of a photograph you find of a place where you fell in love or where you caught the biggest fish of your life. Here and there an insect rose.

Jack had managed to drop a canoe in here, and we got into it. As we pushed off, Jack said, "The trick to catching these brook trout is to keep the fly and the line running straight toward the reel."

When I was first learning to catch trout on flies, I read somewhere that it was always a good idea to fish any water before I stepped into it, and now, from a canoe, I dropped the fly onto the water just ten or fifteen feet away. As the fly fluttered down (it was a Hornberg), a brook trout cleared the water, arching completely out of it, showing its red sides and fins, its somewhat angry mouth. It took the fly on its way *down*. The fish was a little more than a pound. "A baby," said Jack. Christina giggled. Can this really be?

I was certain of few things, but one of them was that Jack didn't joke about this kind of thing. The tug came, not like clockwork exactly, but with a weight that kept me alert. The trout were beginning to get a little red, and although they were not fire-engine red, they were getting pretty pink. Their sides had speckles, just as I had been dreaming of during bad moments, and they had some small, ruby-colored spots surrounded with a blushing ring. The color reminded me of those distant lights in New York when Christina and I would get away to that land and Fish Cabin. I held the fish upside down so that they were still as I took the hook out, and then let them go, the fish slipping into the depths of the pond and leaving a slippery, empty sensation in my hand.

We flew home at dusk, the ponds below looking like mirrors. It was a little cold in the evening, and we needed the woodstove in the cabin. There was an ax outside by the woodshed, and when I picked it up, I touched the edge: It was sharp as a razor. Jack McPhee all over. The edge of the blade was the same color as the pond at dusk.

The next day we fished a bigger pond. There was a little wind when we started fishing, but it was not bad. As we paddled out in the canoe that Jack had left here, it looked to me as though there were some caddis flies on the water, and as I tied on an imitation, the fish began to rise. These were not small fish—most of them being two pounds or more—and for a moment I had the sensation of an optical illusion, the fish rising up and down, hanging in the air, like a horse on a merry-go-round. It was like being in a cauldron of fish.

The sensation of this was enhanced by the wind. The chop of the surface of the pond was not bad, but it was there, and the water didn't have the usual photographically perfect reflection of the shore, but a green color of two shades at least, a darker green on green, and here and there the caddis flies emerged, creamy and moving with a kind of itch. The difficulty was calming down, in not striking so much as just letting the fish take the fly. Not much more was required than raising the tip of the rod, just a bit. More than that seemed to do one of two things: It ripped the fly out of the trout's mouth as it dived, or it broke the fish off. What I liked here was seeing the fish: large, big bellied, with bright spots and with a slight purple cast to them. They were heavy, enormous fish. Jack watched, not smiling exactly, but more with the air of a man who was having a pleasant suspicion confirmed. He got this kind of fishing all the time.

"That's a good one," he said. "Oh, yeah. Look at that one."

We flew back to the cabin at dusk. Christina and I were in the rear, next to a set of tandem controls, which moved as though some unseen hand was flying the plane. The ponds below had the color of a blue-pink mirror. Jack said, in an offhand way, that flying and catching brook trout put him in touch with some "pretty big things." He just said it. Well, what is one to make of a man like Jack? In the evening, in Emerson, I read that the "ethical character so penetrates the bone and the marrow of nature as to seem the end for which it is made . . . " It was the thing I wanted to bring home, and which I tried to. From time to time I will think of Jack, or the memory of a man at the controls of an airplane, who, with a small chuckle of delight, pointed out a bear down below, feeding in raspberries of late August.

From time to time Jack sends me a note, and he will say, "You remember that pond we fished where there was that caddis hatch? Had good fishing up there. Very good. When are you coming back?"

4

One of the things about such fishing is this: When it is that good, it spoils you for some water that is a little closer to home, but only a madman would allow this to last for long. We came home in late summer. It got hot, but I knew of a dam in the Green Mountains that released water from the bottom of its reservoir, and a fisheries biologist told me that there were brook trout to be caught, even in August, if you hiked up to the stream just where it came out of the dam. As I went, in the dusty heat of late summer, which seemed almost like mist, I thought, "Maybe it is not a good idea to think too much, or to try to make sense out of things. Maybe the wise thing is just to come up here to fish for brook trout."

I started at the top of a pool, which had that green and tea-colored look to it that is like a headline announcing the presence of brook trout, and down below it I saw what I thought was a dog, a black one. But then it seemed to me that the dog was a long ways away, and even then it looked pretty big. No, I thought, that's not a dog, but a bear, large and black, laboring in the heat, coming out to drink from the stream, its side bright with sunlight. It was like magic, one thing turning into another (a dog morphing into a bear), and it reminded me of a phone call I received just after we had come back from Maine.

Bill, the FBI agent, said, "Hey, you won't believe this."

"What?" I said.

"The guy who was sending you those letters?" he said.

"Yeah," I said. "What about him?"

"We got him," he said. "He was pulling the same stunt in Burlington. He was carrying a gun when we caught him."

What the letter writer had done, after threatening people in Burlington, was to demand that they rent an apartment and put some food and some money into the icebox of the place they had rented. The FBI was there, wiring the place for sound, when the guy walked in.

"See?" said Christina. "It all works out. You worry too much. You've got to learn to take it easier."

"Uh-huh," I said. "What do you suggest?"

"Go fishing. That's what you are thinking, isn't it?"

"It crossed my mind," I said.

So, I stood in the stream, watching the bear, which was fat on berries of summer, its fur glossy in the sun. It looked up at me and then turned and ran into the shadows of the woods.

Six

*F*riendships are often formed while fishing. While I know of many good cases of this happening, I wasn't catching brook trout when the best example took place, although this experience is bound up with some mysterious aspect of my experience with brook trout.

I had a chance to go to the equatorial Pacific some years ago. The chance came in the middle of winter, when it was twenty below in Vermont, and a magazine asked if I would like to do some exploring. Well, what could I say? No?

Kosrae is a small island in the Eastern Carolines, a part of Micronesia, and I had heard about it from a man who told me that a friend of his, a lawyer, had gone out there after law school and had never come back.

It is hard to realize how much of the world is made up of water, the amount of which is a reassuring prospect for a fisherman. But while it is difficult to come to terms with it, flying across the Pacific is as good a way as any to try to get an idea of how much there really is. The plane droned on. Half of it was filled with cargo behind a webbed partition, and the other part was filled with passengers, many of them islanders who had gone to Hawaii to get medical treatment. Below there was an enormous circle of blue water. The hours went by. The circle stayed the same, and the scale of it after a while began to suggest some other method of measurement aside from hours and miles: The frankly unknowable comes into play, and this naturally leads to humility and the contemplation of the infinite.

Eight hours, by jet, west of Honolulu, the plane landed on a short airstrip. It was a lot shorter than anyone would think a jet could land on, and we came in with the sensation of trying to stop a car when a traffic light suddenly turns red. I got out, into the tropical light, which fell like rain. On the side of the runway was a mangrove swamp, and beyond the swamp was a reef, the mist of the breaking waves there filled with a rainbow. I stayed in a hut on the beach, a thatched one, and in fact there were only five or six beds on the island for outlanders. In the next thatched hut (a real hut . . . this was not a resort), a woman had come from France to drink herself to death, and what I heard each morning, just at dawn, was the sound of her opening her first beer, which she drank like orange juice before switching over to something stronger. Every now and then when I went down to the beach, I saw her on her porch, looking at the rainbow in the mist over the reef. She nodded and waved, and then went back to her drinking, doing so like someone digging postholes.

I met a man by the name of Todao. He was short, had the dark hair and eyes of the islanders, and he had a stammer. He spoke a little English, and we got to talking about fishing. I tried to describe New England trout fishing, and how people there caught trout on small flies, on some pretty small ones, too. For instance, on a #20 hook sometimes. I demonstrated how big a #20 hook was. He stammered with disbelief, but his manners were so perfect, and he was so dignified, he said nothing aside from this, "You and I will go fishing. I'll show you how we do it here."

I agreed, yes. We would go the next day. Then I turned and went along the path back toward the thatched hut where I was staying. The jungle on one side of it was a series of greens, a deeper green gloom on another darker yet, and here and there, from an opening in the canopy, leaves were covered with the gold film of tropical sunlight. In the distance I always heard the sound of the waves breaking over the reef. The trade winds blew, constant, hot, and always in the same direction.

In the morning, I woke to the sound of my neighbor's first beer, and when I went into the damp and gold light of dawn, just at six, she was already there, looking at the reef, the distant white and blue of the ocean. The path led away from the beach, through the shades and green gloom of the jungle.

Todao had a boat, a fiberglass one that had been made in Japan, and it had the basic shape that is seen all over the world: a small cabin for shelter, a deck in front, a cockpit behind. The deck was blue and the hull was white. Todao was waiting for me when I got there. He had his fishing things, which amounted to an enormous ball of string and a lure about the size of a tennis shoe with some feathers attached, double hooks coming out below. He had an assistant, too, a boy of about fourteen, who looked as though he had had a hard night, and to prove it, he went to sleep as soon as we were outside of the lagoon, and he stayed asleep until we had caught a fish.

We went along the coast. The sun rose. What I recall is the mangrove swamps, the shaggy tops of palm trees, the color of the water, which was a blue I have only seen in the middle of the Pacific, and, of course, the sunlight, which came down with such force that it made me feel I had been slapped. The boy's feet were splayed out in a V, and they rocked back and forth as the boat labored in the chop. Todao tied his lure to his ball of string, which looked as though it was a collection of pieces that had been used to tie up boxes from a department store. Surely, though, it had come from some other source. The nearest department store was in Japan, I guessed, by any standards a decent trip by jet.

We worked farther out, on the other side of the reef, the sun hitting me like something poured from a bucket. I wore sunglasses, and when I took them off, it was like coming out of a movie theater in the middle of an August afternoon. Todao had some coconuts, which he cut open with a machete, and the milk was cool and sweet in that solid light. Todao stammered when he spoke.

I sat in the shade for a while, losing myself in the swaying of the boat, in the physical sensation of the heat and light. Todao picked up the line, which was drawn tight into the swells behind us, and said, "Wau."

"Wow?" I said.

He shook his head.

"Wau," he said. "A fish. Wau-wa-wa . . ."

I came out and we stood side by side. He played it onto the ball of string, doing so with a constant patience. The fish stayed deep, the line zinging into the water, moving from side to side. Todao pulled the fish's head out of the water, and then he gaffed it. We dragged it on board, all six feet of it, silvery and flopping in the chop of the Pacific. Todao was a little nervous. I was shaking as though I was reeling in those enormous brook trout on Jack McPhee's pond in Maine. We stood over the glinting fish, which must have weighed sixty pounds, maybe more. Todao looked up and smiled. You see? I don't know about those little flies, he seemed to be saying, but I do know about this.

The instant, though, that we had caught this fish, or that he had caught it and I had helped him pull it on board, he stopped stammering. Just like that. We were friends, having done this thing together. When we turned back and went along the coast of the island, where the shaggy, somewhat dreary palms hung in the light, or when we went along the mangrove swamp, he pointed out a bird, or the way the water broke over the reef. No stammer. It was as though we had been friends for years, and I know that if I showed up tomorrow morning on the island where he lives, he'd say without a stammer, "You remember the Wau? Had to be sixty pounds, don't you think?"

I have noticed this relaxation and trust often among fishermen who have had a good day together. Not large or overwhelming, just a small, dependable comfort. The next morning, hearing that sound of my neighbor's first beer, before she started on her brandy, I thought, Yes, given how things can be, that small comfort isn't bad to have.

Seven

*Y*ear before last I went salmon fishing for the first time. Eric West, a man who is my wife's uncle, and one of the few gentlemen I have ever met, had rented a house on the Restigouche in New Brunswick, and he invited me to spend a few days with him. Eric is a man with a charming smile, a sharp wit, and blue eyes that are capable of an almost infinite number of expressions, from bright and joyful understanding to utter contempt. He has a frank approval of reality, and over the years, through fishing, we have become friends.

The house we stayed in was on the water, and while it was possible to reach it by car or by all-terrain vehicle, the best way was by canoe. Eric's son, Ben, and I arrived on the bank of the Restigouche, where a guide was going to pick us up. This was just before evening and the Restigouche was dark green with streaks of silver around the rocks that stuck up out of the current. It was a stream of medium size, about thirty yards across, and here and there it had long glides. At dusk a layer of mist formed on the surface of the water, and it was out of this island of fog that the guide appeared in a canoe. Ben and I put our things into it. Then the guide turned it upstream, using a small outboard engine, and we disappeared into the mist.

The house Eric had rented was a log building that was at the top of a hundred steps or so that came up from the river. The place had a porch, a living room with a fireplace, a couple of bedrooms, and a kitchen. Originally it had been built by a nineteenth-century sugar baron, and now it was rented out to salmon fishermen.

We fished from a canoe. The way this worked is that there would be three of us together, the guide in the stern, one fisherman in the middle, and one fisherman in the bow. We worked the stream round robin: The guide anchored the canoe and then stood up and cast to one side and then the other, making longer and longer casts, and then the fisherman in the middle stood up and did the same, and then the man in the bow took his turn. It is a meditative and yet demanding way of fishing: There is a certain tension in that the guide is always trying to show off, to cast farther, to handle the entire fly line. I was just interested in catching salmon, although for reasons not clear to me, I was handling a fly rod better than I ever have, before or since. We fell into a regular rhythm, casting longer and longer distances, coming to the limit of what we could do, and then passing the rod to the next fisherman. When we had all fished a piece of water, the guide let the canoe downstream another forty feet or so, and we started again. In the evening, the mist rose, the color of it having a silver cast that reminded me of a salmon. In fact, after hours of casting, there is not much that doesn't remind the salmon fisherman of a salmon.

You could see the salmon, though. They moved into a pool and rested for a while before moving on. First of all, they are hard to see, because they are so perfectly colored, and then, of course, I had not ever looked for something as large as this. When I saw the first one, I thought there was a mistake of some kind. Surely, that couldn't be a fish, could it? There were times when you cast over the salmon, and nothing happened. The flies were gaudy, sometimes looking like a diminutive game bird, a pheasant, say, but gaudy or not, you let them swing over the fish's nose. Nothing happened. You tried again, and then again. Changed patterns. The fish sulked and ignored your flies in a way that seemed indistinguishable from dismissal. Its disdain was almost regal.

Fishing from a canoe allowed us to get very close to the fish. I saw one in the rubble of the stream and cast over it, once, and then again. The thing that surprised me was the sound: The salmon took the fly with a *tock!*, a sound that I couldn't quite place, but which seemed like something from a dream. It was like knocking a knuckle against a violin, but I had never played a violin, thank god, and so I knew that this was not the source of the most intimate of associations. I was still considering this when the salmon made its run: straight downstream, the reel making a sound like it was going to come apart, simply shatter into bits of graphite like a tire blowing up on the highway. The guide moved the canoe to the side of the stream and I got out, trying to play the fish, the creature jumping and revealing itself in a shivery spasm, hanging in the air as though it could exist there, too, and then falling back into the river and running again. The line had too much tension on it, which I knew was a bad thing. About midway into the backing, the monofilament fouled. The salmon broke off and kept right on going, jumping there in the silver current.

Still, the next day, with the reel carefully rewound, I heard that *tock!*, the sound coming again with that haunting familiarity, dreamlike, close to something that I knew was out of my own experience—profound, too, like someone knocking on the coffin one will occupy one day. *Tock!* This time the reel didn't foul, although I learned that what they say is true: Figure two minutes of playing time for every pound of salmon you catch.

At night, Eric looked at me, his blue eyes saying, "So, what do you think about catching these fish?" and at the same time laughing, too, since he knew what I thought about it. He laughed quietly, as though having something he knew all along confirmed. "Here," he said. "How about a drink?"

I slept with the window open, and down below I heard the sound of the river, which made a constant hush, although it wasn't like the wind, or other sounds that vanish into the background, but something at once constant and yet always noticeable—more like a bird singing than anything else. I could even smell the water. The memory of that *tock!* seemed to be right on the edge of the sound of the river, as though this sound existed in the mist or in the silver chop that streaked away from the boulders in the current. Where, I thought, where have I heard that before? The moon was out, and down below, when I looked out the window, the surface of the river was dark, although in the middle of it there was a streak that looked as though it had been made out of nickels, lined up like fish scales. Then I got back into bed. Maybe the memory of this sound was just excitement or a kind of déjà vu. I shrugged. I turned over and tried to sleep and realized what it was. That noise of the salmon taking a fly was an amplified echo of those sounds I had heard years ago on the Mongaup, when I had fished a pool there and had heard the brook trout make that watery *snap.*

Eight

*T*his year has not been a good year for fishing, at least not where I live. I have a little more time to fish now. My older daughter is away at college. My younger is in high school and will be leaving soon. So, this last spring I was looking forward to going back to some streams I have fished over the last twenty-five years. But floods in the spring instantly combined with heat to produce low water, and by June stretches of rivers looked like pools of mercury. As fishermen grow older, they seem to develop a pessimism derived from bitter experience, from days ruined by rain or wind, or by high water or some other unexpected event. This pessimism has a way of clouding one's vision: Such an attitude expects the worst, and, of course, such expectations are easily proved correct.

One of the beauties of fishing, or of spending time in the natural world, is being surprised when you least expect it. For instance, I live near the Connecticut River, which is where I go sculling. It was the thing that kept my weight down so as to take more fishing gear and food to Maine years ago. But the thing that is hard for the sculler is wind, and recently, when I was coming downriver at the end of a long, hard row in the wind, I thought, "This river is never forgiving. It is always tough like this, and that's that." Just as I thought this, I came around a point and into some of the glassiest, smoothest water I have ever rowed in. It was like gliding over a piece of green silk. So, having had this experience, you'd think that I would be more alert to the possibilities of pleasant surprises.

As I say, the fishing was not good this last season. But at the end of it, with inertia born out of the frustration of having had too many days of spring and summer turn into moments when it was obviously better to stay home, I decided to go one last time to one of my favorite spots.

This place is at the top of a mountain, and it is a reservoir. It is about three miles long, maybe more, and at the north end of it there is an inlet. It is not much of a stream, but the reservoir is deep, and I have had good fishing here in the past. The best way to get to this spot is by boat. A friend of mine, Dave Albright, has a boat, and in the early part of October we took it up to the lake.

Dave is a physician and he likes to go fishing to get away from his practice, which includes being a medical director of a local health center and working in an emergency room one night a week. There are occasions when things get pretty rugged in the emergency room, and he has good reason to want to get away. These days what I do as a novelist and the work I do for some film producers often leaves me with that faraway look in my eyes that can only be fixed by a day on a decent stream. Still, as I say, the fishing had been lousy this last year.

So we took the boat up to the lake. From the south side of the lake, you can see some peaks, which at this altitude at this time of the year have a color like the tip of a soldering iron, or like the most orange lipstick you can imagine. These colors are reflected in the water. We got into the boat and started going north. It was not very windy, but in Vermont at this time of the year we have frosts in the morning. It was cool. Overhead we had an osprey, and a couple of loons were out in the middle of the lake. No one else around.

At the north end, where the inlet is, we started fishing, but we weren't doing much. I noticed a pair of waders in the boat. I put them on and walked over to the shore, so I could get closer to where the water was a little faster. I have noticed over the years that this is a great place to catch brook trout, some of them of good size, just when the light is off the water and when there is a little hatch of mayflies or caddis flies. In the mud close to the stream, there were the tracks of moose, and what looked like the tracks of wild turkeys, too. The thing, though, that really distinguished this place was the silence, which was enhanced by the lack of direct sunlight. The wind had died down, and the water was still.

I sat down and began to think about some trouble I was having. In the writing life there is always something that isn't quite right—not, of course, that this is any different from any other kind of life. And what was this season's worry? Well, I have published nine novels, and this year I had gone through another change, just like at the green house, in what and how I wrote. When you change, it is hard to get this across to readers and to publishers. I realized that there wasn't much I could do about this. Time would do the trick, as it always did. But I sat there, going through the possibilities. I could do this. I could do that. Maybe. In the water, just where the current flowed into the lake, I saw a little ring. Was that an insect or a fish? There's a bubble.

I had on a little nymph, and I dropped it into the ring, waited for a minute, and twitched it. Stripped it a little, with an anxious, nervous movement. *Bang.* The place was stiff with brookies. They made a silver splash in the water that seemed covered with a film of red and orange. They were brightly colored, too. Their mouths were large, wide open, as they waited for me to remove the nymph. I sat down and waited for them to start rising again. They did.

At this time of the year, when the sun goes down, the temperature drops, and in this drop, you can feel the coming of winter and a hint of those nights when it is twenty below and when, if you are outside, the snow squeaks when you walk on it. So, I came home, still seeing that silver splash in the orange reflection of the leaves and thinking, Yes, that's right. The surprise always comes at the worst moment of pessimism.

I learn something every season. This year it was this: There is something else to these endeavors, something more profound and difficult to describe than just catching fish, something that has to do not only with being alive, but with the impulse toward persisting in the face of difficulty. And how does one persist? Well, I am not certain, but I know this. Relaxing in the middle of the worst (which is a refusal to despair) is part of it. From time to time the natural world bestows one of its pleasant surprises, and I have learned to be alert to them.

During important events in my life, I have often gone fishing for brook trout. What I got out of this was not just the absence of what was confining or upsetting, but the presence of another quality altogether: These fish are forever associated in my mind with the depths of thankfulness for good fortune, just as they always reminded me of beauty and a sense of what may be possible after all. Fish rise. The rings spread. When I catch them, they make a splashing crown of water. For one instant, everything stops.